NIGHTLIGHTS

by Paul Paolilli and Dan Brewer   pictures by Alice Brereton

Albert Whitman & Company
Chicago, Illinois

Outside our window,
away in the night,
is a world full of wonder,
so quiet—
so bright.

We see endless stars,
the sweet Milky Way,
poured from a dipper
on a velvet display.

There's moonglow, a moon print,
as a cloud tags along.

It's a whole moon,

a half-moon,

a sliver,

now gone!

Look! A meteor shoots out of the blue—
a wink, a blink,
and our wish can come true.

Nightlights near,
nightlights far,
nightlights surprise us wherever we are.

In firefly meadows,
we're seated front row
for the blinking and whizzing—
of a fireworks show!

A campfire crackles;
we hear laughter and smile—
songs in the woods,
sounds of the wild.

Whose eyes do we spy
perched high in a tree?
Owl eyes!
Catching moonlight to see!

In a beam and a burst
and a sudden spark—
a distant light flashes
and brightens the dark.

It's a lighthouse,
a hero's house,
saving ships at sea.
Fluorescent waves
in a light parade
are marching endlessly.

Nightlights near,
nightlights far,

nightlights guide us wherever we are.

From high on a hill,
a thousand lights shine—

sprinkled like sugar
or all in a line.

The city lights sparkle
from town to town,
and we count them like diamonds
tossed on the ground.

There's a railroad crossing—
a rush of light—
a train on its way—
soon out of sight.

Streetlamps and footlamps,
wherever we roam,
make puddles of light,
neon stepping stones home.

Now on our front porch,
a cheerful light,
welcome and warm,
calls us in for the night.

Lights out in the kitchen,
lights off overhead;
a light on the staircase
leads us to bed.

Tucked in and warm,
Papa winks a *good night*,
wishes sweet dreams,
then turns out the light...

And there in our room
till morning's first call
is our own little nightlight,
hugging the wall.

Nightlights near,
nightlights far,
nightlights with us wherever we are.

To Betty and Deane Nuss, for the light of my life.—PP

To Rudy, and to my mom, for all the light and love she gives.—DB

To Anna and Anthony Paolilli, for all that they gave us.—PP & DB

To my lovely mom!—AB

Library of Congress Cataloging-in-Publication
data is on file with the publisher.

Text copyright © 2017 by Paul Paolilli and Dan Brewer
Pictures copyright © 2017 by Albert Whitman & Company
Pictures by Alice Brereton
Published in 2017 by Albert Whitman & Company
ISBN 978-0-8075-5622-1

Printed in China
10 9 8 7 6 5 4 3 2 1 LP 22 21 20 19 18 17

Design by Jordan Kost

For more information about Albert Whitman & Company,
visit our website at www.albertwhitman.com.